Female Body Image

A Hot Issue

Rosemary Genova DiBattista

Enslow Publishers, Inc.

40 Industrial Road   PO Box 38
Box 398   Aldershot
Berkeley Heights, NJ 07922   Hants GU12 6BP
USA   UK

http://www.enslow.com

For Mom and Dad, with love and thanks

Library of Congress Cataloging-in-Publication Data

DiBattista, Rosemary Genova.
    Female body image : a hot issue / Rosemary Genova DiBattista.
        p. cm. — (Hot issues)
    Includes bibliographical references and index.
    Summary: Details the effects that the media has on body image,
describes how women adorn and alter their bodies to conform,
and explores how to develop a positive body image, despite what
society considers ideal.
    ISBN 0-7660-1812-1
    1. Feminine beauty (Aesthetics)—United States—Juvenile litera-
ture. 2. Body image—Juvenile literature. 3. Self-esteem in
women—United States—Juvenile literature. 4. Women in popular
culture—United States—Juvenile literature. 5. Surgery, Plastic—
Juvenile literature. [1. Beauty, Personal. 2. Body image.
3. Self-esteem. 4. Surgery, Plastic.] I. Title. II. Series.
HQ1220.U5 G46   2002
305.4—dc21

                                    2001006251

Printed in the United States of America

10 9 8 7 6 5 4 3 2 1

To Our Readers: We have done our best to make sure all Internet
Addresses in this book were active and appropriate when we went to
press. However, the author and the publisher have no control over and
assume no liability for the material available on those Internet sites or on
other Web sites they may link to. Any comments or suggestions can be
sent by e-mail to comments@enslow.com or to the address on the back
cover.

Illustration Credits: AP/Wide World Photos, pp. 18, 20, 28, 33, 51,
52; Corel Corporation, pp. 9, 25, 43; Dover Publications, pp. 16, 40;
Skjold Photographs, pp. 1, 12, 36, 55.

Cover Illustration: Skjold Photographs.

Contents

Chapter 1

The Female Self-Image

As a young girl, Yvonne did not give much thought to her appearance. She dreamed about being a famous author. Yvonne also wrote in her diary about traveling the world and having adventures. But as her body changed, so did Yvonne's dreams.

Between the ages of thirteen and fifteen, Yvonne grew nearly six inches and put on over forty pounds. At five feet six inches, Yvonne weighed 150 pounds. Such growth is natural in an adolescent, but Yvonne felt it was a problem. She wanted to look like the women she saw in magazines and in movies. Yvonne wrote that she wished she could be "slim and sylph-like."

When she entered high school, Yvonne grew more dissatisfied with her looks. She got a stylish new haircut, but she still felt large and clumsy. She was invited to a luncheon for young poets, but she hesitated about going. In her diary, she wrote that the red dress she had picked out made her look like an elephant, and she called herself a "fat, crude beast." She wrote: "I wonder if anyone in the world has ever hated herself as I hate myself?"

Yvonne believed that dieting would be the answer to all her problems. At fifteen, she wrote, "I'm so tired of being fat!" She was determined to lose thirty pounds, "or die in the attempt." She began to weigh herself regularly and wrote down everything she ate. Certain foods, like fried chicken and ice cream, would tempt her. Her parents would insist that she eat, and Yvonne would get angry. She admitted to her diary that she sometimes wrapped her meal in her napkin and fed it to her dog. Yvonne went to the extreme measure of eating no more than fifty calories a day. (A growing teenage girl needs around two thousand calories a day.) She allowed herself only lettuce, carrots, tea, and soup. This diet made her so ill that one day she fainted.

Dieting became such an obsession with Yvonne that she competed with her friends to see who could lose the most weight. They discussed the subject constantly. Yvonne thought that a new body would give her a new image. But this new image had to be thin, or Yvonne would not be satisfied.[1]

Allegra's Story

Allegra remembers standing in front of her mirror as a five-year-old, thinking that she "was far too heavy." She began dieting at the age of six. For several days in a row she would eat nothing but fruit. When she became hungry, she would eat again, but feel guilty about it. Allegra's mom did not keep fattening snacks in the house, because she did not want her daughter to gain weight. Sometimes, at school or at a friend's house, Allegra would eat snacks like ice cream and chips. But when she got home, she would make herself throw up.

By the time Allegra was ten, she was bulimic.

Bulimia is an eating disorder characterized by purging—taking laxatives or throwing up after meals, often several times a day. Allegra eventually stopped eating altogether and became anorexic by the age of twelve. Anorexia is an eating disorder characterized by fasting, or not eating at all. She was five feet seven inches and weighed 130 pounds. To Allegra that seemed very fat. By the time she was fourteen, she had grown two inches. She had also lost a good deal of weight.

Allegra's body began shutting down. She suffered hair loss and her periods stopped. Her fingers and toes would turn blue, and she felt cold all the time. Whenever she stood up, she felt as if she would pass out. For Allegra, the worst thing about having an eating disorder was "feeling isolated and alone all of the time." She knew that she could die from eating so little. Frightened, she began eating again but was also purging as many as fifteen times a day.

At the age of eighteen, Allegra was still battling eating disorders. She had been hospitalized twice, and her condition improved. She worked hard to recover from her eating disorders, but found it difficult, because she still had trouble with her body image. In her own words: "It's hard to wake up every morning and be afraid of looking in the mirror."[2]

Body Image and Self-Image

The girls whose stories you have just read have one important thing in common: a negative body image that led to self-destructive behaviors. But Yvonne and Allegra were of two entirely different generations. Yvonne was born in 1911. As a young woman in the 1920s, she wanted a slender figure popularized by the "flapper look." Allegra was born more than seventy years later, but her concerns were exactly the same. Both young women suffered from a poor body image.

What is body image? And why does it have such an impact on how girls (and boys, too) feel about themselves? Body image is made up of three parts: the mental picture we have of our physical selves; how we believe others perceive us; and how comfortable we are with our own bodies.[3] These components really cannot be separated. If, for example, a girl believes she is fat, she will think that others see her as fat. A girl who thinks her nose is too big or her hair is too curly might believe people are focusing on that feature when they look at her. These doubts make girls uncomfortable with their physical selves and may lower their self-esteem. A girl who does not accept her body will have a difficult time accepting herself.[4]

A recent survey conducted by Brown University indicated that the majority of girls between the ages of twelve and eighteen were unhappy with their bodies.[5] A different study, conducted by The Renfrew Center in Florida, revealed that nearly 80 percent of seventeen-year-old girls did not like their bodies.[6] Where would so many young women get the idea that they are fat or unattractive? The answer is as close as the nearest magazine.

Body Image and Body Ideals

More than two thirds of the girls in the Brown University survey reported that pictures of models in magazines influenced their idea of the perfect body.[7] Television, film, posters and print ads are also filled with images of women who are very thin, with

*B*ody image includes the mental picture we have of our physical selves.

flawless skin, perfect hair, and great clothes. Every day, young girls are exposed to a female ideal that is impossible to live up to.

Women's bodies come in all shapes and sizes. But the women shown on television, in movies, and in magazines are generally slim. (In fact, many actresses and models are actually underweight.) Girls compare themselves unfavorably to the slender actresses and models they see in the media. Even girls who are of a healthy weight for their body type have a hard time accepting their bodies when

Do You Like Your Body?

Use the following checklist to help distinguish between mild body dissatisfaction and a more serious body image problem. Ask yourself if you are:

- Unable to accept compliments.
- Constantly comparing your body to others.
- Happy or unhappy according to how you think you look.
- Habitually criticizing yourself.
- Seeking constant reassurance from others regarding your looks.
- Prone to describe your body with negative words, like fat, flabby, disgusting, ugly.
- Dissecting your body into parts, like large rear, huge thighs, thick waist, small chest.
- Weighing yourself frequently, afraid of gaining one or two pounds.
- Turning down social invitations because you think you do not look good enough.[8]

faced with such images. These images tell us what we are "supposed to" look like. In reality, few of us look like supermodels. But many young girls feel unattractive or even worthless if they do not.

In our society, being thin is associated with beauty, power, and health. For many girls and women, thinness is a measure of self-worth. Girls grow up with a fear of getting fat. At a very young age, children develop a negative attitude toward those who are overweight. Adults, too, make judgments about people who are heavy. Fat people are the target of jokes and often the victims of prejudice. When girls say they "feel fat" or "feel ugly," what they might actually be saying is "I don't like myself" or "I don't know how to cope with my real feelings or problems."[9] For many girls, these feelings are temporary. But for some girls, the answer to all problems lies in being thin. To what lengths will girls go to alter a negative body image?

Striving for Perfection

There are many ways to change our appearance. For example, women may use makeup to enhance their facial features. They may adorn their bodies with jewelry or fashionable clothing. Less common— and more dangerous—adornments include tattoos or piercings. Practices to alter body image may include extreme dieting or extreme exercising. Perhaps the most dramatic way to change the body is with plastic surgery, which carries medical risks. Yet more and more women are willing to undergo surgery in their quest to be beautiful. Even among teens, plastic surgery is on the rise.[10]

The actresses and models that young girls try to emulate sometimes adopt unhealthy practices in

*D*oubts about how she looks to others can lower a young woman's self-esteem.

order to be thin and beautiful. Their weights often fall below what is considered healthy. Some have ended up with eating disorders. Many have breast implants or other plastic surgeries. These women go to extremes to conform to society's current body ideal. And many adolescent girls will do the same.

The chapters that follow detail the effects that media images have had on body image. They will also describe how women adorn and alter their bodies to conform to certain ideals. Slowly, however, our society seems to be moving toward accepting a more realistic female body image and embracing different ideas of beauty. Young women can grow up with a positive body image, despite what society considers ideal.

Look at any group of women. Short or tall, thin or fat, dark or fair-skinned—the variety is endless. Once you have noted how the bodies look, then think about what those bodies can *do*. The female body is capable of bearing and feeding a child. It is also strong enough to win a marathon or build a house. Yet its curves and softness are what make us uniquely feminine. Your body is a miracle of nature, and it should be treated that way—with respect and pride.

Chapter 2

The Historical Image

It may be surprising to learn that a thin body was not always considered ideal. At various times in history, different body shapes were idealized. Primitive civilizations created very round stone figures of women with large breasts. These figures represented fertility and emphasized maternity and childbirth. The ancient Greeks prized muscular, athletic forms. The Romans, however, valued thinness. In fact, it has been suggested that the Romans "invented" bulimic behaviors. After huge feasts, the Romans would force themselves to vomit so that they could consume even more food—an unhealthy practice then, as it still is today.

In the West, a slender form was valued well into the Middle Ages. The women's clothing of the period reflected this ideal. The garments flattened the normal curves of the woman's body to create the illusion of thinness. By the fifteenth century, however, a more rounded form was considered attractive. In fact, from about 1400 through 1700, plumpness was considered "both erotic and fashionable."[1] European paintings of this period often depicted large women with prominent curves. Sixteenth-century painter Peter Paul Rubens was well known for his plump female nudes. Even today, the term "Rubenesque" is used to describe a full-figured woman in a flattering way. Plumpness, for both men and women, was actually a status symbol well into the twentieth century, because a full figure meant you were well fed.

The Nineteenth-Century Female

A larger body ideal remained in vogue throughout the nineteenth century. In both Europe and America, women strove to look full-chested and broad-hipped. By the 1880s, plumpness was considered beautiful.[2] Doctors encouraged young women to eat heartily, as plumpness was considered a sign of good health. Under their clothing women wore corsets, restrictive garments which laced tightly across the torso. Corsets created an unnaturally tiny waist and exaggerated the woman's chest. The bustle, a stiff, padded garment, was worn under skirts to make a woman's hips look larger.

One of the most admired women of that era was a music hall singer named Lillian Russell. In the 1880s, she was considered the height of femininity. Russell was known for her lovely skin and blonde hair, as well as her generous curves. In fact, Lillian Russell was seen as the ideal woman of the age—and she weighed nearly two hundred pounds.[3]

By the last decade of the nineteenth century, a new ideal had taken hold in America. The so-called Gibson Girl, however, was not a real woman. She was a figure that appeared in magazine illustrations, the creation of artist Charles Dana Gibson. The

Gibson Girl was tall, with broad shoulders, long legs, and a tiny waist. Her body was described as having an "S-curve," with a chest that thrust forward and high hips. The S-curve was an extreme look that could only be achieved by wearing a painful corset. Still, young women all over the United States yearned to look like the Gibson Girl. Fashion magazines advertised soaps, clothing, and other products that promised a Gibson Girl look. Women who could afford such products bought them eagerly.

The Flapper

By the turn of the twentieth century, women were slowly growing more independent. Young women in particular were beginning to rebel against the Victorian ways of the previous era. For example, nineteenth-century women generally had long hair. Young women in the new century defiantly "bobbed" theirs. (A bob is a chin-length haircut still popular today.) Remember Yvonne? She bobbed her hair just before she entered high school in the hopes of looking more stylish. Many girls started smoking or following silly fads. One such fad was to wear their rain boots unbuckled. When they walked, their boots made a flapping sound, and the term "flapper" was born.

Young women who were flappers came of age in the 1920s. Journalist Laura Fraser described them as "impulsive, flirtatious, jazz-dancing young women."[4] Flappers did not wear corsets that emphasized their curves. Instead, they wore waistless, sheath-style dresses to give the body a straighter line. Large-chested young women wore fabric "flatteners" under their clothing to bind their breasts. A boyish look was so desirable that many American girls began a habit that persists today—constant dieting.[5] (Dieting means restricting calories in order to lose weight.) One might say that today's slender ideal all began with the flapper, more than eighty years ago.

From Rosie the Riveter to Marilyn Monroe

A slimmer body remained in vogue in the years before World War II. The film stars of the 1930s reflected this. Stars such as Katharine Hepburn, Bette Davis, and Myrna Loy were slim, even by today's standards. Fashions of the era, which included jackets and trousers, tended to hide curves. Such masculine fashions were indicative of women's new independence. They were also far removed from the corseted look of the previous century.

*T*he flapper of the 1920s had short hair and wore straight, low-waisted dresses.

By the early 1940s, America had entered World War II. Many women held jobs to support the war effort. There is a famous poster of a factory worker called "Rosie the Riveter." Rosie's sleeve is rolled up to reveal a strongly muscled arm that looks masculine. Even women's fashions were influenced by the war. Jackets and blouses often came with large shoulder pads, giving their wearers a more masculine look. After

World War II, however, there were many cultural changes. Women's roles began to shift again, as did ideas about what a woman's body should look like.

Once the war was over, women were expected to take their places at home. They were also expected to be—and look—more feminine.[6] By the late 1940s and early 1950s women's fashions emphasized femininity, and a new ideal was also emerging. She was large breasted and curvy, and looked plump compared to today's movie stars. This figure was exemplified by Marilyn Monroe, a film star of the 1950s.

Though Marilyn Monroe has been dead for many years, her image is very much alive. Her face still appears in art, posters, and ads. With her blonde hair and generous curves, Monroe was considered the "sex symbol" of her time. She had a whispery voice and a childlike way of speaking. She played many "dumb blonde" roles, but this was a label that would eventually bring her distress. Journalist Laura Fraser has noted that "the annoying association between blondes, breasts, body fat, and brainlessness continues even today."[7] Like Lillian Russell before her, Marilyn Monroe represented a plumper and rounder female figure. In the coming decades, however, the female ideal would shift once more. By the 1960s, thin was once again "in."

Twiggy, Hardbodies, and Waif Chic

From the twenties through the fifties, female film stars were representative of American ideas of beauty. By the sixties, however, the fashion industry was growing in power. Also powerful were the images of the women wearing the clothes—the models. It is

Miss America's Changing Image

Female body ideals have grown thinner since the early years of the twentieth century. Researchers at the Johns Hopkins School of Public Health compiled data on Miss America contestants from 1922 through 1999. Using the weight and height of each of the winners, the researchers determined their body mass index, or BMI. (BMI is calculated through a mathematical formula that evaluates weight in relation to height.) Their study found that earlier Miss America winners had BMIs within a range that is considered normal, between 20 and 25. Over the years, however, there has been a general decline in their BMIs, with some as low as 16.9. (A person with a BMI number under 18.5 is considered undernourished.)

The Johns Hopkins researchers have expressed concerns that pageant competitions may have an effect on young women's decisions about weight and diet, because it promotes a too-thin female ideal.

The two Miss Americas shown below illustrate this trend. Both were five feet nine inches tall; however, Miss America 1968 (left) weighed 135 pounds, while Miss America 1986 weighed 114 pounds.[8]

really models—and those who designed clothes for them—who created "the vogue of extreme thinness" that persists today.[9] One of the earliest (and skinniest) of these models was Twiggy. Twiggy's real name was Lesley Hornby. At five feet seven inches tall and weighing ninety-five pounds, it is easy to see how she got her nickname. Twiggy's flat-chested, boyish look echoed that of the flapper. Twiggy's look was an impossibly thin standard for most women.[10]

It was also in the sixties that another version of female beauty emerged. The political and civil rights changes of that decade led to the slogan, "Black is beautiful." For the first time, African-American fashion models were being featured in magazines and ads. And a greater variety of racial and ethnic looks were considered beautiful. Women of different ethnic backgrounds were beginning to see faces in the media that resembled their own. This was at least one positive effect of the fashion industry.

Twiggy led the trend toward the thinner models and actresses of the seventies, like Farrah Fawcett and Cheryl Tiegs. It was also at this time that a fitness craze was emerging in the United States. Swimsuit models appearing in ads and magazines were not only slender, but also more muscular. By the eighties, *Jane Fonda's Workout*, in book and video form, was a best-seller. Women who had dieted to get thin now felt pressured to work out as well. Many women began using weights and machines to create a hard, sculpted look. Though being fit is a worthy goal, many women took it to extremes. They exercised not to maintain good health, but to imitate a new ideal, the "hardbody."[11]

Too much exercise, or exercising improperly, can lead to physical injuries. Many women are well

*L*ike a flapper, Twiggy, the premier fashion model of the 1960s, had short hair and a boyish figure. (But unlike a flapper's, her skirts were extremely short!)

aware of the dangers of extreme dieting or exercise. But the desire to emulate an ideal can often overcome good sense. This issue came to the forefront in the nineties, with the emergence of another look—the waif.

A waif is literally defined as "one who is lost, without a home; especially a homeless child."[12] Among models, the "waif look" was epitomized by model Kate Moss. At five feet seven inches, and approximately one hundred pounds, Moss was indeed thin. But she was also often photographed with a sad, distant look on her face. Her extreme thinness gave her a childlike air. The waif image presents a weak and vulnerable female—not an ideal most women choose to emulate. Though a slim body is still considered ideal, the era of the waif—and other extreme looks—appears to be over.

This history of body image in America reveals a changing pattern. Sometimes plump, sometimes lean, body ideals seem to shift with each generation. They are influenced by our culture and our politics, but most powerfully, by our print, television, and film media.

Chapter 3

The Media Image

The image of the Gibson Girl appeared on everything from magazine covers to soap packages. In later decades, movie and television actresses represented the height of female beauty. Today, young women are still bombarded with images of thin, beautiful women held up as ideals. They appear in magazines, on television, in films, and on public billboards. But when young women look at such images, what do they see? Do they see themselves and their friends? Or do they see an unreal and impossible standard of beauty?

Real or Ideal?

The lean, angular bodies of fashion models are presented as an ideal. A five foot ten inch model who weighs 110 pounds has a body type that is often chosen to model clothes or sell products. But most women are not supermodels. A woman's body is typically made up of 25 percent fat. The soft, fatty tissue that develops during puberty is necessary for growth, development, and reproduction.[1] In fact, the average American woman is about five feet four inches tall and weighs between 140 and 150 pounds. More than half of all American women are between size 14 and 24. Those women represent what is *real*, rather than ideal.

Women who consider themselves overweight may be perfectly healthy, according to their body mass index, or BMI. The BMI uses a mathematical formula to evaluate weight in relation to height. The BMI is expressed in a two-digit number that generally falls between 12 and 34. In adults, a BMI above 27 indicates obesity, but in children and teens, a BMI of 30 may still represent normal weight gain.[2]

The majority of media images show thin women with very low BMIs. Women and girls who view enough of these images come to accept them as the norm. In fact, most models weigh approximately 23 percent less than the average woman.[3] What used to be an extreme has become a standard of beauty. And it is a standard that girls measure and judge themselves against.[4]

Girls look at such media images and have unrealistic expectations. They think that they should be that thin and possess certain characteristics to be beautiful. But they are looking at retouched and airbrushed photographs. They are seeing women who are photographed in the most flattering light after hours of hairstyling and makeup. With new technology, computer-enhanced and even computer-generated images are appearing more frequently, but they present a "virtual" picture. In reality, the "perfect" women in magazine ads do not even exist.[5] But the media would have women believe that they do, for a very simple reason—it sells products.

FAKE
Computerized

Body Mass Index

Body mass index (BMI) is calculated as follows:

(weight in pounds / height in inches / height in inches) x 703

So, someone 62 inches tall weighing 120 pounds has a BMI of 21.9, since (120/62/62) x 703 = 21.9.

Keep in mind that because children and teens are still growing, their BMIs may be higher than would be healthy for an adult.[6]

"You Can Never Be Too Thin. . ."

"You can never be too thin or too rich." In some ways, that expression has become a motto for our times. It is a message that is sent over and over again in advertising. Being thin is equated not only with beauty, but also with the good life. Ads for luxury cars feature a thin, beautiful model behind the wheel or in the passenger seat. Commercials for diet products and low-fat foods suggest that being thin will make you happy. According to sociologist Sharlene Hesse-Biber, "the thin woman gets the goodies. The man, the car, the glamour."[7]

Hesse-Biber has written about girls with eating disorders. She believes the media plays a major role in how girls see themselves. Media images of thin, glamorous women seem to imply that thinness and beauty equal success.[8] Young girls have anxieties about their bodies. And companies that market diet and beauty products play upon those anxieties.[9] A new lipstick promises beauty; a diet shake promises thinness. Such products seem to be quick fixes for the doubts we all have about our looks. What is more, the advertisements seem to imply that buying a particular product will make women happy as well as beautiful.

Ads for food products also exploit women's fears about getting fat. A recent milk campaign featured thin, beautiful celebrities like Tyra Banks and Neve Campbell admitting that even they worry about getting fat. (The solution to their "problem" was to drink skim milk.) The message is that even seemingly perfect women still obsess about body weight and appearance.[10]

It is not only advertising that affects how young women perceive their bodies. Movies and television programs regularly feature thin women; when overweight women appear, they are subjects for scorn and humor. Gwyneth Paltrow and Julia Roberts, who are very slender actresses, wore "fat suits" in recent films to show their characters before they lost weight—when they are usually the butt of jokes. In television shows such as *Friends*, all three female leads are very slender. It is interesting to note that the character of Monica, played by Courtney Cox Arquette, was supposedly fat as a teenager. Flashback episodes show Cox wearing padding and makeup to look very heavy. And Rachel, the character played by Jennifer Aniston, is humorous in the flashbacks because she has a large (pre–plastic surgery) nose. The message is very clear, and it is not being lost on young women: Perfect features and body are crucial to happiness.

The Effects of Media Images

Much research has established the effects of media images on girls and young women. A 1995 study published in *Psychology Today* revealed how fashion magazines affect women. A group of women spent three minutes looking at pictures of very thin models. Afterwards, 70 percent of them felt ashamed, guilty, or depressed about their bodies.[11]

More recent research at the University of Toronto included young women of college age. More than one hundred female college students were asked about their body image. Their answers ranged from slightly negative to generally positive. One week later, they were shown a series of magazine ads featuring models. Researchers then asked them the same questions they had one week earlier, but their answers had changed. The women's attitudes toward their bodies were now described as "hostile" and "depressed."[12]

Younger girls are also affected by images of very thin women. In 1998, Harvard researchers studied more than five hundred girls between the ages of eleven and eighteen. They found that 59 percent of the girls were dissatisfied with their bodies. Sixty-six percent wanted to lose weight. However, only 29 percent of the girls were

*A*dvertising sends the message that luxury products and beautiful women go together.

Teens Talk Back to Media Messages

Bluejean magazine asked teens: What messages in the media do you think need to be changed and why? Here is some of what they had to say:

"The media is filled with false messages: one of the worst is that material goods will bring happiness. People must find true happiness inside themselves." Tiffany, age 16

"The media targets young women, centering the focus on the so-called, 'stereotypical girl,' with the perfect face, figure, and personality." Kristin, age 19

"I think the media needs to tone down the emphasis it places on looks. Young girls see an unattainable image. . . .Emphasis needs to be taken away from what is on our outsides, and placed on who we are on the inside. I think the media has a responsibility to offer alternative sources of information for girls that don't bombard them with advertisements full of messages on how they are supposed to look." Anne, age 18[13] actually overweight. The Harvard study also looked at girls who were frequent readers of fashion magazines. This group was much more likely to diet to lose weight. And many of the girls in the study admitted that magazine images influence their perception of body ideals.[14]

If there is any doubt about the power of the media, consider the effect of television on the young women of the Fiji Islands. Ideals of beauty vary from culture to culture. In Fiji, the ideal body for a woman is plump and round. Before marriage, Fijian girls go through a period of heavy eating. Plump, curvy brides are considered attractive—or at least they were until fairly recently.

In the mid-nineties, satellite television brought American programs to remote areas of these islands. Fijian girls began seeing actresses like Heather Locklear from *Melrose Place*. In 1999, a survey of sixty-five Fijian teenage girls revealed that American television was influencing their body image. Girls who watched television three or more nights a week reported feeling "too big" or "too fat." Two thirds of the girls had gone on diets. The girls, whose average age was seventeen, said that they wanted to look like the actresses they saw on television. Fifteen percent of them admitted to vomiting to try to control weight. Significantly, only 3 percent of them had vomited to lose weight before 1995—the year television arrived.[15]

Despite the power of current media images, there are some encouraging trends. Plus-size models like Emme are featured more frequently on television and in magazines, as are women of different ethnic backgrounds. Female athletes like Venus and Serena Williams appear in ads flaunting strong and

*C*alista Flockhart, star of the television show *Ally McBeal*, exemplifies the super-thin ideal for actresses that has been in style recently.

powerful bodies. Benetton clothing ads, for example, include people of diverse races, backgrounds, and appearance. Images of disabled women are also beginning to appear, both in print and on screen. And though thinness is still prized, a greater variety of female beauty is finally emerging in the media.

Chapter 4

The Decorated Image

Nearly all human beings adorn themselves in some way. There is no known culture that does not use some form of body decoration. Adornment may include painting, piercing, tattooing, reshaping, or scarring the body. People in different cultures decorate their bodies in various ways. Often such adornments are used to conform to an ideal of beauty.

In our culture, women adorn themselves with jewelry, cosmetics, and hair color. They may use tinted contact lenses to change eye color. Both men and women have their teeth whitened. They may use body glitter or wear temporary tattoos. A few even choose to get permanent ones. Body piercing, too, is a growing trend. All these adornments have their roots in history.

Cosmetics and Body Painting

Body paint, or makeup, is made of removable substances. Powders, dyes, and other pigments are used to transform appearance or enhance beauty.

How people use cosmetics reflects their culture's idea of beauty. At one time, for example, Japanese women blackened their teeth—a quality that their culture considered beautiful.

It is not certain when people first began using cosmetics. However, evidence from ancient Egypt dates the practice to about 10,000 B.C. Cosmetic trays with pigments still in them have been found in Egyptian tombs. Throughout most of history, there is evidence of the use of cosmetics. The ancient Babylonians curled their hair. The Greeks dyed theirs blond. The Romans whitened their teeth using pumice stones. Ladies of the Renaissance lightened their skin with white lead, a poisonous substance. Some became sick as a result—all in the name of beauty.

The urge to enhance beauty still persists. Today, the cosmetics industry is big business. In 1996, for example, women in the United States spent more than one billion dollars on makeup. Currently, about 90 million American women over the age of eighteen wear makeup. It is projected that by the year 2007, that number may reach 95 million.[1] That represents a lot of lipstick and mascara. Why do so many women wear makeup?

The purpose of cosmetics is to highlight certain features. Social psychologist Dr. Martin Skinner believes that most cultures use cosmetics as a way to accentuate their features to increase sexual attraction.[2] But there may be more to it than that. Sheila Rossan is a psychologist who believes that, for women, using makeup "is a part of our identity [and a way] that you can change your body image. . . ."[3]

We live in a world that prizes beauty (though

what is *considered* beautiful is different in different cultures). Research has shown that when meeting someone for the first time, the visual impression carries the most weight. Some women use makeup to create the impression they want to make.

Max Factor, a large cosmetics company, conducted a 1998 survey of more than ten thousand women. Many respondents said that using makeup made them feel more attractive and confident. The survey also revealed that the use of cosmetics is highly individual. Younger women often sought a natural look. Some professional women chose a bolder look, perhaps to create an impression of power. According to Rossan, women often change looks. "Make-up is not just how we present ourselves to others," she says, "it is how we feel about ourselves."[4] Using cosmetics, however, is a personal choice. Some women do not use cosmetics for religious reasons. For others, the look they are most comfortable with is simply a clean face.

Body Paint and Tattoos

Certain kinds of body art go beyond the use of cosmetics. In many cultures both men and women have decorative designs painted or tattooed on their bodies. One common type of temporary design is created with henna, a red dye that comes from plant extract. Henna is painted on the skin and allowed to dry, leaving a dark red stain. Henna designs, also known as *mehndi*, are considered markers of beauty. In countries such as India and Morocco, henna painting is considered a female art form. The designs usually designate important events in a woman's life, such as marriage. Unlike permanent tattoos, however, the markings eventually fade.

In recent years temporary tattoos created with henna have become popular in the United States. Many people, including some celebrities, sport "skin jewelry," henna designs that resemble bracelets, rings, and anklets. Such designs last about six weeks and provide a safer alternative to traditional tattoos.

Permanent tattoos are created by puncturing the skin with a sharp instrument filled with pigment or

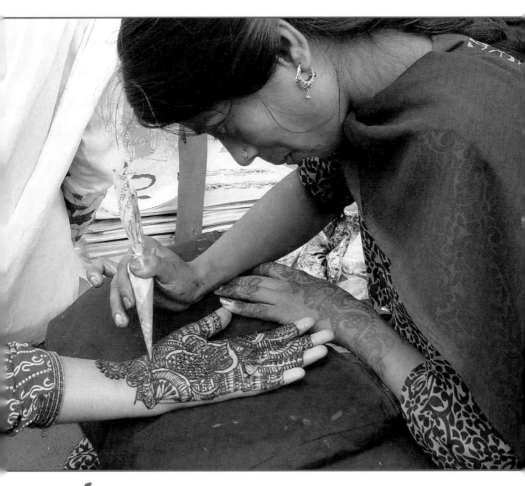

*I*n India, temporary tattoos called *mehndi* are applied to the skin, often as a part of festivals or family celebrations.

dye. The needle is inserted through the outer layer of skin, or epidermis, into the second layer, or dermis. The modern method of tattooing employs a tattoo gun. Such guns "shoot" the ink under the skin with electrically powered needles.

Tattooing is a growing industry in the United States, particularly among teens. A recent study indicated that one in ten teens had a tattoo. And more than half the kids surveyed said they were thinking about getting one.[5] Those teens might be surprised to learn that tattooing is actually a very old art.

In Polynesia, elaborate tattoos have traditionally been a sign of manhood. Certain designs indicated high rank. Even today, tattoos in Polynesia are a respected tradition. In Japan, on the other hand, tattoos were frowned upon. Wealthy Japanese associated tattoos with certain professions that they considered to be lower class.

In the United States, tattoos have long been associated with sailors and gang members. For most of the twentieth century, tattoos were considered signs of defiance in the United States. But now tattoos have taken on a different meaning—they seem stylish and trendy. Tattooed rock stars and celebrities make the practice seem acceptable. But one rock star, Guns 'N Roses lead singer Axl Rose, warns teens: "Think before you ink."[6]

For one thing, the procedure requires parental consent for anyone under eighteen. (In seven states, tattooing is not legal at all, even for adults.) Even if they have parental permission, teens need to know that getting a tattoo is risky and painful. Large ones may take several hours to complete. The process has been described by one teen as "a long, drawn-out, burning pain."[7] In addition, some people may have allergic reactions to tattoo dyes.

Inexperienced tattooists pose other problems. Using unsterilized equipment increases the risk of serious health problems such as AIDS, hepatitis B, and tetanus. Tattooists may also use the gun improperly. If so, the electric needles may penetrate fat and muscle tissue, causing excessive bleeding. Even under the best of conditions, the tattooed area stays tender for a long time.

Basically, tattoos are permanent. Though laser surgery is available to remove tattoos, the process is costly and painful. Older methods like excision (cutting the skin) or dermabrasion (sanding the skin) may leave scars or some permanent color behind. The tattoo a teen chooses may represent only a passing interest. But the consequences of such a decision may last a lifetime. Teens who think they want a tattoo must consider such a decision very carefully. In the meantime, lots of temporary tattoos are available. You can get the look—without the pain, the risks, or the expense.

Face and Body Piercing

Piercing involves inserting a needle or other instrument into the skin to create an opening for jewelry or another decorative item. The area is pierced in such a way to allow the healing of tissues around the opening. In most cultures, the most commonly pierced areas are the soft tissues of the face and ears.

Like tattooing, piercing is an old art. Small figurines showing piercings have been found in Inca and Mayan burial sites. Such piercings are also time-honored traditions among African and Indian peoples. Piercing may mean different things in different cultures. In some, piercing may be part of a coming-of-age ceremony. In others, it may indicate wealth and status.

Simple ear piercing has long been common in the United States. But current trends include multiple ear holes, eyebrow, lip, tongue, navel, nipple, and genital piercing. Like tattooing, body-piercing businesses are growing rapidly. Body piercing is popular among some teens. However, most piercers will not perform the procedure on anyone under eighteen without parental consent.[8]

Teens may want to pierce their faces and bodies for a variety of reasons, such as fashion, affiliation

with a certain group, or rebellion. Adolescents are always looking for ways to set themselves apart from older generations—namely, their parents. Unusual piercings still have shock value. Some teens may think they are expressing their individuality. But like tattooing, piercing has risks.

Piercers who are not well trained may not take the necessary health precautions. Equipment that is not sterile may spread HIV, hepatitis B, or other infections. Poor quality jewelry can lead to

*S*ome people express their individuality by getting tattoos and face or body piercings, such as this young woman with a reindeer tattoo.

A Piercee's Bill of Rights

Every person being pierced has the right:

1. To be pierced in a scrupulously hygienic, open environment, by a clean, conscientious piercer wearing a fresh pair of disposable latex gloves.

2. To a sober, friendly, calm, and knowledgeable piercer, who will guide him or her through the piercing experience with confidence and assurance.

3. To the peace of mind which comes from knowing that his or her piercer knows and practices the very highest standards of sterilization and hygiene.

4. To be pierced with a brand-new, sterilized needle that is immediately disposed of in a medical sharps container after use on the piercee alone.

5. To be touched only with freshly sterilized, appropriate implements, properly used and disposed of or resterilized in an autoclave prior to use on anyone else.

6. To know that piercing guns are NEVER appropriate, and are often dangerous, when used on anything, including earlobes.

7. To be fitted only with jewelry that is appropriately sized, safe in material, design, and construction, and which best promotes healing. Gold-plated, gold-filled, and sterling silver jewelry are never appropriate for any new or unhealed piercing.

8. To be fully informed about proper aftercare and to have continuing access to his or her piercer for consultation and assistance with all piercing-related questions.[9]

allergic reactions or infections. And certain piercing sites carry specific risks. Improper piercing of ears may split or tear earlobes. Multiple piercings on the rim of the ear do not heal well and tend to scar. Piercings in the nasal area take a long time to heal. Jewelry may become embedded in the nasal tissue. Piercing the tongue causes the highest risk of infection, since the mouth contains lots of bacteria. Jewelry may be swallowed or cause teeth to fracture. Other risks include numbness, damage to cheek tissue, loss of taste sensations, or slurred speech. Pierced navels may take a full year to heal. The navel area also tends to get irritated and infected from clothing rubbing against it. Nipple piercings may produce scar tissue or infection. The delicate tissues around the genitals are also at a higher risk of infection while the wound is still healing. According to registered nurse Myrna L. Armstrong, "There are virtually no risk-free situations when it comes to body piercing."[10]

For teens who like body jewelry, there are less risky options. Unusual and interesting jewelry is a safe way to adorn the body. For a pierced look, there are clips available for noses. Adjustable "ear cuffs" can be worn on any part of the ear's rim, without the risk of scarring. Some teens wear magnetic jewelry that comes in two parts. They can be worn on the lips, nose, or upper ears and have a pierced look.

Adornment is one way to enhance or change one's appearance and boost confidence. In all cultures, human beings decorate their bodies in various ways. Each culture has its own definition of beauty. But the desire to be beautiful is nearly universal. Unfortunately, it is sometimes so strong that women will endure pain or risk their health—all in the pursuit of beauty.

Chapter 5

The Altered Image

In the attempt to imitate ideals of beauty, many women go further than just adorning their bodies. They attempt to alter them through exercising, dieting, and wearing restrictive garments. Some women even resort to plastic surgery. Unfortunately, in their attempt to dramatically reshape their bodies, many women end up harming themselves.

Some women's bodies are altered because of accidents or problems at birth. Some facial disfigurements, for example, may be corrected with plastic surgery. Other disabilities, such as a loss of a limb, may require a prosthesis, an artificial limb with working parts. Women with disabilities face issues of body image that go well beyond size or weight.

The Corseted Lady

The use of dieting, exercise, and plastic surgery to alter the body did not come into wide practice until the twentieth century. Before that, women relied on restrictive clothing to reshape their bodies. The corset, for example, is a rigid garment designed to tighten a woman's waist.

Back Then

A scene from the 1939 movie *Gone With the Wind* shows the beautiful but vain heroine, Scarlett O'Hara, dressing. The film is set in the nineteenth century, when most women wore corsets. Scarlett is shown holding her breath so that her servant can lace her corset as tightly as possible. Even though she can barely speak, Scarlett wants the corset still tighter. Scarlett's goal was an eighteen-inch waist—no matter how much she had to suffer to get it.

By creating a tiny waist, corsets exaggerate the natural lines of a woman's body, making her chest and hips look bigger. Corsets were made of leather, fabric, bone, and even metal. In fact, the very first corsets were made of steel and worn by Minoan women in Greece more than three thousand years ago. In Western culture, corsets were worn from about the twelfth century right into the early years of the last century.[1] Corsets that were made rigid through the use of steel or bone stays were described as "an agonizing straight-jacket to endure."[2] The tightness of the garment severely restricted a woman's movement, and it even made breathing difficult.

*T*his corset ad from 1922 shows the restrictive garment designed to make a woman's body fit the popular ideal.

Sometimes corsets put so much force on a woman's body that her internal organs were compressed or shifted from their natural positions. Some very tight corsets would cause a woman's ribs to grow into her liver or other organs.[3] The flapper styles of the 1920s, as well as women's new-found independence, helped bring an end to the corset.

A later version of a corset, the girdle, was made of elastic and more flexible materials. In the 1940s and 1950s, many women wore girdles to create a smooth line under their clothing. By the 1970s, however, girdles too were mostly a thing of the past, due to changing fashions and changing politics. The so-called natural look reflected the ideas of a growing women's movement, as well as a desire for more comfortable clothing. Many women still wear undergarments that slim the body. Control-top pantyhose, spandex slips and underwear, and padded bras are all ways women try to alter their shapes. Although today's slimming undergarments do not pose the health hazards of old-fashioned corsets, they are often uncomfortable.

Exercise Obsession

In the early part of the twentieth century, women's increased participation in sports promoted a more comfortable style of dress. Women were now swimming, playing tennis, bicycling, and participating in team sports.[4] Athletic women had slimmer figures, so a new way to alter bodies emerged—exercise. By the 1980s, "working out" had become a mania, and an entire industry formed around physical fitness. Many women embraced the idea of strenuous exercise—but often for all the wrong reasons. The aim of exercise should be to stay fit and healthy. But *compulsive exercising*

many women (and men) use exercise as a means to alter their bodies. Exercising for good health is an admirable practice. But too much exercise puts a strain on the body and may cause injuries. And when exercise becomes an obsession, women may find themselves battling the genuine disorder of compulsive exercising. This is sometimes called "exercise bulimia."

Compulsive exercising is a form of purging. It may exist on its own or overlap with eating disorders such as anorexia or bulimia. People who suffer from this disorder may exercise from two to six hours a day. They will exercise in any weather and feel guilty about missing even a day. They will continue to exercise despite illness or injury. Exercise becomes more important than family life and social life.[5]

The effects of compulsive exercise can be devastating. Serious physical injuries, such as bone fractures, torn ligaments, and sprains can occur. Over the long term, exercise bulimics may end up with osteoporosis (loss of bone density), heart complications, and fertility problems. Young women may stop menstruating or experience hair loss.[6] What should be a healthy practice—exercise—is taken to a dangerous extreme. Those who exercise compulsively often act compulsive in other ways, as well. They will often obsess about a pound lost or gained. In fact, compulsive exercise often goes hand in hand with another harmful practice—compulsive dieting.

Dieting

Diet books of the late 1910s and early 1920s emphasized calorie counting. Since then, fads like the Hollywood diet and the grapefruit diet have gone in and out of fashion. In the early 2000s, the Atkins Diet of the 1970s once again became popular, as did the Zone Diet. Programs like Weight Watchers, Jenny Craig, and Nutri-System also became enormously successful. The diet industry is big business in the United States—more than $50 billion a year. While the media promotes an ever-thinner ideal, the diet industry's profits grow.[7]

Such diets promise dramatic results. They are heavily advertised, often with celebrities endorsing them. As a result, people buy diet books, packaged diet foods, and diet pills and shakes. Many join diet programs like Weight Watchers. But do all these diet products and programs work?

Different diets and programs vary a great deal in how healthy and effective they are. Diet programs that stress eating reasonable portions of a variety of

*W*hile exercise is necessary for good health, the effects of overexercising can be very serious.

healthy foods are more effective. Such programs create better eating habits and make it easier to maintain a healthy weight. A good diet program should also encourage moderate exercise to keep the body fit and balance calorie intake.

The Effects of Dieting

Most people think of dieting as simply reducing calorie intake. They also associate dieting with skipping meals, giving up rich foods, and feeling guilty about what they eat. When people find themselves unable to stick with a diet regimen, they give up. Then they feel guilty and unhappy and start dieting all over again in a cycle of "yo-yo dieting." This pattern of repeated dieting, weight loss, and weight gain often leaves the dieter weighing more than he or she did to begin with.

In fact, a recent study conducted by Stanford University's School of Medicine found that teens who dieted regularly tended to gain weight instead of lose it. The four-year study tracked nearly seven hundred girls in a California high school. By the end of the study, the girls who were regular dieters had gained more weight than girls who were not. Researchers believe a pattern of yo-yo dieting may be responsible for the weight gain.[8] How does this happen?

Dieting increases hunger and thoughts about food. When excessively hungry, the dieter becomes more susceptible to rebounding and overeating so-called forbidden foods. Breaking a diet can also cause feelings of low self-worth. In fact, "the diet mentality can take a toll on both body and soul."[9]

Perhaps the most harmful effect of dieting is its association with eating disorders. It is estimated that

Do You Have An Eating Problem?

Here are some things to look for if you think you or a friend might have a problem.

- You stop eating or feel guilty when eating certain foods.

- You don't like to eat in front of other people and may even stop going to fun events because there might be fattening foods.

- You weigh yourself a lot and feel fat even when you aren't.

- You often count calories and/or fat grams and worry about what you'll eat next.

- You purposely don't eat for awhile, and then overeat and feel guilty.

- You occasionally purge by making yourself vomit, using laxatives, or overexercising.[10]

5 to 10 percent of all adolescent girls and women in the United States suffer from some kind of eating disorder. These disorders may include anorexia, bulimia, or binge eating.[11]

Eating disorders often begin with dieting. When those diets do not work, people may begin practicing unhealthy behaviors such as fasting or purging. Once an eating disorder is established, a girl faces many health risks. Her periods may stop, her growth may be stunted; even her heart may be adversely affected. It is estimated that 10 percent of long-term anorexics actually die from the disease. Younger girls are also beginning to show symptoms of eating disorders. In recent years, the average age of diagnosis of eating disorders has dropped from seventeen to fourteen. Even children as young as ten may be afflicted.[12] As one young woman, Elizabeth, said, "I began to diet, starve, and compulsively exercise at the age of eight or nine. . . . There was constant pressure to be thin."[13]

Plastic Surgery

Some teens opt for a more extreme method than dieting to change their appearance: plastic surgery. ("Plastic" in this sense means "formative.") Plastic surgery was first used during World War I to reconstruct the faces of soldiers who were disfigured in battle. Reconstructive plastic surgery is still used in cases of injury or to correct birth defects. This type of surgery is medically necessary and covered by insurance. Cosmetic, or aesthetic, plastic surgery is elective. In other words, a person chooses to have her face or body altered through surgical means. Such procedures are costly. Most are not covered by health insurance.

Only about 3 percent of all plastic surgeries are performed on teens. However, the *number* of teens getting cosmetic surgery is increasing. For example, in 1998, breast enlargements, or augmentations, for girls eighteen and under nearly doubled, from 978 to 1,840. Rhinoplasties, or nose jobs, remain the number one procedure for teens. In 1998, the number rose from 5,519 rhinoplasties to 8,074.[14] Whether or not they actually have plastic surgery, more teens regard it as a way to alter body image.

Dr. Ann Kearney-Cooke is a physician and scholar with the Partnership for Women's Health at Columbia University. Dr. Kearney-Cooke recently conducted an Internet survey of four thousand teenage girls. Almost half of the fourteen- to eighteen-year-olds said they were not satisfied with their bodies. A third of the teens said they were considering some type of plastic surgery. Dr. Kearney-Cooke believes that media images of flawless bodies and faces affect how teens view themselves. "Teens feel so much pressure to be instantly perfect," she says.[15] It is this pressure to be perfect that leads some teens into doctor's offices—and onto operating tables.

Some Common Procedures and Their Risks

Plastic surgery is not only a drastic option, but also a risky one. Some plastic surgeons will not perform elective operations (except in the case of accident reconstruction or birth defects) on any patient younger than eighteen. The American Society of Plastic and Reconstructive Surgeons stresses physical development over age. Operating on a feature that is not fully developed could interfere with growth. Also, a teen must be emotionally mature enough to understand and accept the risks involved.

Adolescence is a time when the sense of self is still developing. For teens, that sense of self is strongly tied to body image, and some may see plastic surgery as a solution. Some common procedures performed on teens include breast reduction, breast augmentation, and rhinoplasty. All require some form of anesthesia, which in itself carries risks. There are also individual risks associated with each procedure.

Breast Reduction. Girls with overly large breasts may feel self-conscious about their appearance. They may also have physical problems, such as back pain, poor posture, or rashes. As Lori, one young woman who chose to have breast reduction surgery, said, "I was uncomfortable. I felt totally unattractive and I was so tired of the heat rashes under my breasts and not being able to do the things I used to enjoy."[16]

Breast reduction must be performed under general anesthesia and usually requires at least a one-day stay in the hospital. The return to normal activities usually takes four to six weeks. Risks from this surgery include loss of body fluids and excessive bleeding.

Breast Augmentation. Unlike breast reduction, breast augmentation is not performed for medical reasons. The choice to have breast implants is usually aesthetic. (One exception is breast augmentation that is needed after a mastectomy, or breast removal.)

Breast implants were once made of silicone. Silicone implants caused serious health problems, including leakage and excessive scarring. Today's implants still have a silicone envelope, but are filled with saline instead. There are still risks involved in this procedure, however.

Implants may prevent a mammogram (a test designed to detect breast cancer) from providing a clear reading. It is also possible for even saline implants to rupture, and further operations may be required if implants shift.

Possible complications include infection, fluid accumulation, and excessive bleeding and scarring.

Rhinoplasty. Rhinoplasty, also known as a nose job, alters the nose's shape through surgery. Among teens having plastic surgery, rhinoplasty is the most common procedure. Though they are commonly performed, nose jobs require a very skilled surgeon to get the best results.

Rhinoplasty may be performed under local or general anesthesia. Using a small instrument that resembles a chisel, the surgeon will modify the nasal skeleton by making a series of small fractures of the nasal bone. (The black eyes that are typical of this surgery occur as a result of these fractures.) While healing, the nose must be packed with surgical gauze to hold its new shape. Complications from rhinoplasty may include nasal bleeding, nasal obstruction, and sinus problems. Infections following this surgery are rare but dangerous.

Liposuction. In liposuction, excess fatty tissue is suctioned from beneath the skin. It is generally performed on the abdomen and thighs, though it is sometimes used in face-lifts and chin-tucks. Anesthesia may be general or local. Surgeons insert a hollow, wandlike instrument called a cannula through incisions in the skin. The cannula is moved through the tissues, where it breaks up fatty deposits. A vacuum device then suctions out the material.

Liposuction is the most risky of all plastic surgeries, with a death rate of one in five thousand. Risks include stress to the heart, nerve compression, blood clots, and infection. Also, the results of liposuction may only be temporary, because the body tends to create fat deposits in other areas. The Food and Drug Administration (FDA) has in fact raised several concerns about the safety of liposuction.[17]

Chapter 6

The Changing Image

Today there is a heartening trend emerging in the media. Women of varying sizes, as well as those who are not conventionally "beautiful," are appearing in magazines, in film, and on television. Women's sports have helped promote a stronger, more athletic female ideal. Today's young women are seeing a wider variety of female body types.

The issue of body image is beginning to receive a great deal of attention. The rise of eating disorders among young women has prompted researchers to look for solutions. As a result, there are now many self-help and self-acceptance programs available to girls. These programs help girls learn to accept their bodies and themselves.

The Real Woman

Television mothers have traditionally been slim, pretty, and well dressed—even while doing housework. In the 1990s, however, Roseanne Barr broke the mold of the television mom. Large, loud, and fearless, Roseanne's character was often abrasive, but in many ways she represented the "average" woman. And her body type reflected that woman.[1] There have always been large women on television. But more often than not, the "fat lady" was the butt of jokes. Now actresses like Emme, Camryn Manheim, Kathy Najimy, and Queen Latifah are featured on television in positive ways. So too are actresses who do not necessarily look like fashion models, but project other qualities, like intelligence, wit, or strength.

Heather Mills was a fashion model until an accident changed her body—and her life—forever. In 1993, Mills had just returned to London from a trip helping war victims in Bosnia when she was hit by a police motorcycle. Her left leg was severed below the knee. Though Mills believed her modeling career was over, she learned to wear a prosthesis. One year later she founded the Heather Mills Health Trust, which recycles used prostheses to amputees in many nations. Today Mills still models, skates, plays tennis, and continues her charitable efforts.[2]

Queen Latifah has appeared on television shows on the Fox network and hosted her own talk

*A*s the media has begun to show acceptance of more diverse female body types, actresses such as Camryn Manheim of *The Practice* have been featured in serious roles.

show. Latifah, who was born Dana Owens, has always had a strong self-image. By the age of twenty, she was a rap star and comfortable with her body. Also named to *People*'s 1999 list of beautiful people, Queen Latifah considers herself a strong, sexy woman. "I'm cool with myself," she says.[3]

The Athletic Ideal

Soccer players like Mia Hamm and Brandi Chastain have plenty of curves, but they are defined by muscle. The late Florence Griffith-Joyner would appear at track meets with elaborate hairstyles and perfectly manicured nails. But her powerfully muscled body proved that strength and femininity were not a contradiction in terms. Female athletes are more focused on what their bodies can *do*, rather than on what they look like.

*F*lorence Griffith-Joyner, a track star who died in 1998, illustrated both femininity and strength.

Former volleyball player Gabrielle Reece is six feet three inches tall and weighs 170 pounds. For a time, Reece was a model and weighed less. But she did not feel as healthy and fit as she does now, weighing twenty-five pounds more. When she works out, she likes the idea that she is training to get stronger, not skinnier. For Reece, "The true criterion for looking beautiful is looking healthy."[4] Runner Lynn Jennings advises girls to take pride in strength.

When she competes, she likes feeling bigger and stronger than the women she is running against. Her body, she says, "is a source of confidence for me because I know I can power past [smaller women]."[5]

Paths to Self-Acceptance

Though young women are exposed to a wider variety of body types nowadays, the pressure to be thin or look perfect is still strong. How can teens respond to that pressure and maintain a healthy body image and self-esteem?

Currently there are many doctors, educators, and counselors who are working to help girls with issues of body image. The Harvard Eating Disorders Center has designed a program called *Full of Ourselves: Advancing Girl Power, Health and Leadership* for teen and preteen girls. The program helps girls focus on good health instead of body image. It emphasizes girls' personal power and overall well-being.

Full of Ourselves was developed to help girls improve their self-esteem and confidence. Girls who participate in the program learn healthier eating habits and how to deal with teasing about weight. Older girls who complete the program then serve as mentors to younger girls. Any interested school or youth group can adopt this program by contacting the Harvard Eating Disorders Center.[6]

Sandra Susan Friedman is an educator and therapist and the author of *When Girls Feel Fat: Helping Girls Through Adolescence*. After working with girls who had eating disorders, Friedman shifted her focus to prevention. She created a program called *Just For Girls*, an open discussion group. The program

Learning Self-Acceptance

Accepting the body we have is not always easy. To do that we must look closely at our beliefs about beauty and body image. Use the questions below to get you thinking about body image issues:

- **What do the words "fat" and "thin" mean?** What do you associate with these terms?

- **Do you get contradictory messages about food from television or magazines?** Are there ads for diet aids alongside information about healthy eating?

- **What does a healthy body look like?** A strong body? A beautiful body? Which do you want?

- **Do you think there are different types of beauty?** What are they? What do you feel when you see pictures of models? Of a Rubens painting? A female athlete?

- **What makes you forget about your appearance?** When you are spiking a volleyball or talking with a friend, for instance, do you forget that you think your hips are too round or your nose is too big?

- **If you ever feel fat or unattractive, what is really going on?** When was the last time you felt that way? What triggered that feeling?

- **What have you learned at home about being fat or thin?** Do your parents diet? Feel self-conscious about their weight? Tease you?

- **What is it like to be a girl these days?** How do you think your experiences differ from those of boys or girls of your parents' generation?

- **What makes you feel good about yourself?** What makes you proud?[7]

teaches girls how to decode "fat talk." Fat talk is a way for girls to sympathize with each other about body image. But it is also a way for them to openly dislike their bodies. *Just For Girls* helps them get to the issues behind fat talk, whether those issues are low self-esteem, insecurity, or peer pressure. Through role-playing, discussion, and creative activities, girls are able to express themselves in a safe environment.

Friedman says the program provides girls "with an awareness of their own bodies that goes beyond relating to them solely in terms of how they look." Sarah, a seventh-grade student who completed the program, had this to say: "We covered a lot of important issues such as: eating disorders, puberty, families, friends and boyfriends, and women in the media. We also learned that each one of us was great just the way we were."[8]

"Turning Beauty Inside Out"

We are born with only one body. Its shape, size, and weight are determined mostly by genetics. We can put makeup on it, decorate it with jewelry, or adorn it with the latest fashions. We can try to lose pounds from it, overexercise it, or even have a surgeon cut into it. Ultimately, we cannot

*Y*oung women need to learn to like what they see in the mirror and to value themselves for who they are and what they can accomplish.

change it very much, at least not without some risk to it. Our body is our own, not like anyone else's. And it is the only one we will ever have.

Self-acceptance, however, does not come easily. Girls must try to resist the media images and the fat talk. They need to learn to like the face and the body they see in the mirror. They should focus on what their bodies can do instead of how they look. Most importantly, they need to understand that body image is exterior. The New Moon Web site urges girls to "turn beauty inside out."[9] Once the girl inside recognizes her hopes and dreams and knows who she really is, she will learn to like herself better. She will become prouder and more confident—and that is the true source of her beauty and power.

The BodyWise Eating Disorders Initiative,
Part of the Girl Power! Campaign
Office on Women's Health
Department of Health and Human Services
200 Independence Avenue, SW Room 730B
Washington, D.C. 20201
202–690–7650

Eating Disorders Awareness and Prevention, Inc.
603 Stewart Street
Suite 803
Seattle, WA 98101
206–382–3587
800–931–2237 (toll-free information and referral
hotline)

Center for Media Education
2120 L Street, NW
Suite 200
Washington, D.C. 20037
202–331–7833

American Dietetic Association
P.O. Box 97215
Chicago, IL 60678–7215
800–877–1600, ext. 5000

Association of Professional Piercers
PMB 286
5446 Peachtree Industrial Boulevard
Chamblee, GA 30341
888–555–4APP

American Society of Plastic Surgeons
Plastic Surgery Educational Foundation
444 East Algonquin Road
Arlington Heights, IL
888–475–2784

Chapter Notes

Chapter 1. The Female Self-Image

1. Joan Jacobs Brumberg, *The Body Project: An Intimate History of American Girls* (New York: Random House, 1997), pp. 100–104.

2. Allegra, "Share Your Story," *Dying to Be Thin*, NOVA Online, December 14, 2000, <http://www.pbs.org/wgbh/nova/thin/story_001214.html> (January 4, 2001).

3. Mary Alice Collins, "Stranger in the Mirror," *Sarasota Magazine*, vol. 22, December 1999, p. 141.

4. Ibid.

5. "Media Has Major Impact on Girls' Body Image," *Brown University Child & Adolescent Behavior Letter*, vol. 15, May 1, 1999, p. 4.

6. Collins, p. 141.

7. "Media Has Major Impact on Girls' Body Image," p. 4.

8. Adapted from Collins, p. 143.

9. Sandra Susan Friedman, *When Girls Feel Fat: Helping Girls Through Adolescence* (Buffalo, N.Y.: Firefly Books, 2000), p. 56.

10. Barbara Whitaker, "Cut to Fit," *New York Times Upfront*, vol. 132, April 14, 2000, p. 8.

Chapter 2. The Historical Image

1. Thomas F. Cash and Thomas Pruzinsky, eds., *Body Images: Development, Deviance, and Change* (New York: Guilford Press, 1990), p. 85.

2. Lois W. Banner, *American Beauty* (New York: Alfred A. Knopf, 1983), p. 106.

3. Ibid., pp. 156–157.

4. Laura Fraser, *Losing It: America's Obsession with Losing Weight and the Industry That Feeds on It* (New York: Dutton, The Penguin Group, 1997), p. 33.

5. Ibid., p. 34.

6. Susan J. Douglas, *Where the Girls Are: Growing Up Female with the Mass Media* (New York: Random House, 1994), pp. 45–47.

7. Fraser, p. 41.

8. "Is Miss America an Undernourished Role Model?" *JAMA*, vol. 183, no. 12, March 22/29, 2000, p. 1569.

9. Banner, p. 287.

10. Fraser, p. 43.

11. Ibid., p. 44.

12. David B. Guralnik, ed., *Webster's New World Dictionary*, Second College Edition (New York: Simon and Schuster, 1983).

Chapter 3. The Media Image

1. Susan Brownmiller, *Femininity* (New York: Simon and Schuster, 1984), p. 32.

2. William V. Tamborlane, ed., *The Yale Guide to Children's Nutrition* (New Haven: Yale University Press, 1997), pp. 26, 33.

3. Elaine Gale, "Body Image: The Big Picture," *Minneapolis Star Tribune*, December 9, 1997, p. 01E.

4. Susan Bordo, *Unbearable Weight: Feminism, Western Culture, and the Body* (Berkeley: University of California Press, 1993), p. 25.

5. Michelle Card, "Build a Better Body Image," *Total Health*, vol. 15, October 1993, p. 16.

6. U.S. Centers for Disease control, "What Is BMI?" n.d., <www.cdc.gov/nccdphp/dnpa.bmi/bmi-definition. htm> (December 7, 2001).

7. Courtney Young, "Is the Media Dictating Beauty Standards?" *dr.koop.com: Women's Health*, n.d., <http:// digitalcity.drkoop.com/family/womens/feature.asp?id= 4624> (January 17, 2001).

8. Ibid.

9. Joan Jacobs Brumberg, *The Body Project: An Intimate History of American Girls* (New York: Random House, 1997), p. 124.

10. Nona L. Wilson and Anne E. Blackhurst, "Food Advertising and Eating Disorders: Marketing Body Dissatisfaction, the Drive for Thinness, and Dieting in Women's Magazines," *Journal of Humanistic Counseling and Development*, vol. 38, December 1999, p. 111.

11. Gale.

12. Sandra W. Key and Maryclaire Lindgren, "Skinny Models in Ads Cause Immediate Anger, Depression in Women," *Women's Health Weekly*, May 10, 1999, p. 11.

13. "Hear from the Pocket," *bluejean.online.com*, n.d., <http://www.bluejeanonline.com> (March 20, 2001).

14. Alison E. Field, et al., "Exposure to the Mass Media and Weight Concerns Among Girls," *Pediatrics*, vol. 103, March 1999, p. 103.

15. "Fat-phobia in the Fijis: TV–Thin is In," *Newsweek*, May 31, 1999, p. 70.

Chapter 4. The Decorated Image

1. Shannon Dortch, "Women at the Cosmetics Counter," *American Demographics*, vol. 19, March 1, 1997, p. 4.

2. Glenda Cooper, "The Hidden Meaning Behind Your Mascara," *Independent*, Newspaper Publishing, P.L.C., n.c., April 1, 1998, pp. C2, C3.

3. Ibid.

4. Ibid.

5. Carolyn Gard, "Think Before You Ink," *Current Health 2*, vol. 25, February 1999, p. 24.

6. Ibid.

7. Ibid.

8. Myrna L. Armstrong, "A Clinical Look at Body Piercing," *RN*, vol. 61, September 1998, p. 27.

9. The Association of Professional Piercers, "A Piercee's Bill of Rights," n.d., <www.safepiercing.org/billofrights.html> (December 7, 2001).

10. Armstrong, p. 29.

Chapter 5. The Altered Image

1. Doreen Yarwood, *The Encyclopedia of World Costume* (New York: Bonanza, 1986), pp. 109–112.

2. Ibid., p. 110.

3. William Bennett and Joel Gurin, *The Dieter's Dilemma* (New York: Basic Books, 1982), p. 183.

4. Lois W. Banner, *American Beauty* (New York: Alfred A. Knopf, 1983), p. 276.

5. Grail McGinley, "Exercise Bulimia: A New Compulsive Disorder That Can Hurt Women," *Newsday*, April 1, 1996, p. B13.

6. Ibid.

7. Laura Fraser, *Losing It: America's Obsession with Weight and the Industry That Feeds on It* (New York: Dutton, 1997), pp. 55, 56, 60.

8. Bev Bennett, "Teen Dieting Backfires: Study Says Girls Who Diet Face Greater Risk of Obesity than Nondieters," *Newsday*, April 2, 2000, p. B15.

9. Randi E. McCabe, Jennifer S. Mills, and Janet Polivy, "Ditch Your Diet!" *Diabetes Forecast*, vol. 53, January 2000, p. 49.

10. U.S. Department of Health and Human Services, *Girl Power! Page*, n.d., <www.girlpower.gov/girlarea/bodywise/eatingdisorders.index.htm> (December 10, 2001).

11. "Ten Million Women Suffer From Eating Disorders," *Women's Health Weekly*, February 15, 1999, p. 8.

12. Judith Newman, "Little Girls Who Won't Eat," *Redbook*, vol. 189, October 1997, p. 120.

13. Elizabeth, "Share Your Story," *Dying to Be Thin*, NOVA Online, <http://www.pbs.org/wgbh/nova/thin/story_001214.html> (September 27, 2001).

14. Barbara Whitaker, "Cut to Fit," *New York Times Upfront*, vol. 132, April 14, 2000, p. 8.

15. Paula Gray Hunker, "Pressure to Be Perfect," *The Washington Times*, February 1, 2000, p. E1.

16. *Lori's Breast Reduction Journal*, n.d., <http://lorisbrjournal.freeservers.com/index.htm> (September 27, 2001).

17. Alexandra Greeley, "Planning to Look Flab-u-less? Know the Facts About Liposuction," *FDA Consumer*, vol. 34, November/December 2000, pp. 31–35.

Chapter 6. The Changing Image

1. Susan J. Douglas, *Where the Girls Are: Growing Up Female with the Mass Media* (New York: Random House, 1994), pp. 284–285.

2. "Model Citizen," *People*, vol. 51, May 17, 1999, pp. 117–118.

3. "Queen Latifah," *People*, vol. 51, May 10, 1999, p. 176.

4. Gabrielle Reece, "What's the Big Ideal?" *Women's Sports and Fitness*, January/February 2000, p. 70.

5. Megan Othersen and Robert McClintock, "My Body, My Self," *Runner's World*, vol. 28, June 1993, p. 73.

6. "Full of Ourselves: Advancing Girl Power, Health, and Leadership," *Harvard Eating Disorders Center*, n.d.,<http://hedc.org/whatwedo/fullof.htm> (March 14, 2001).

7. "Body image—Parent and teacher guide," *chatelaine.com*, n.d., <www.chatelaine.com> (March 20, 2001).

8. "Just For Girls," *Salal Communications Ltd.*, n.d., <http://www.salal.com/just.html> (March 14, 2001).

9. "Turn Beauty Inside Out: Important Facts," *New Moon Publishing*, n.d., <http://www.newmoon.org/TBIOD/index.html> (March 14, 2001).

Books

Brumberg, Joan Jacobs. *The Body Project: An Intimate History of American Girls.* New York: Random House, 1997.

Davis, Brangien. *What's Real, What's Ideal: Overcoming a Negative Body Image.* New York: Rosen, 1999.

Gadeberg, Jeannette. *Brave New Girls: Creative Ideas to Help Girls Be Confident, Healthy, and Happy.* Minneapolis: Fairview Press, 1997.

Graff, Cynthia Stampler, Janet Eastman, and Mark C. Smith. *BodyPRIDE: An Action Plan for Teens: Seeking Self-Esteem and Building Better Bodies.* Torrance, Calif.: Griffin Publications, 1997.

Graves, Bonnie. *Tattooing and Body Piercing.* Mankato, Minn.: Capstone Press, 2000.

McCoy, Kathy, and Charles Wibblesman. *The New Teenage Body Book.* New York: Berkeley Publishing, 1992.

Schwager, Tina, and Michelle Scheurger. *The Right Moves: A Girl's Guide to Getting Fit and Feeling Good.* Minneapolis: Free Spirit Publications, 1998.

Shandler, Sara. *Ophelia Speaks: Adolescent Girls Write about Their Search for Self.* Thorndike, Maine.: Thorndike Press, 2000.

Sneddon, Pamela Shires. *Body Image: A Reality Check.* Berkeley Heights, N.J.: Enslow Publishers, Inc., 1999.

Internet Addresses

Bluejeanonline.com
<http://www.bluejeanonline.com>

New Moon Publishing
<http://www.newmoon.org>

Women's Sports Foundation
<http://www.womenssportsfoundation.org/cgi-bin/iowa/>

Further Reading